For Snowy the survivor (seven lives left!)—PB

For Prinsi-Minsi—CC

PENGUIN WORKSHOP

An imprint of Penguin Random House LLC, New York

First published in Great Britain by Macmillan Children's Books,
an imprint of Pan Macmillan, 2022

First published in the United States of America by Penguin Workshop,
an imprint of Penguin Random House LLC, New York, 2023

Text copyright © 2022 by Peter Bently
Illustrations copyright © 2022 by Chris Chatterton

Visit us online at penguinrandomhouse.com.

Library of Congress Cataloging-in-Publication Data is available.

Manufactured in China

ISBN 9780593520864   10 9 8 7 6 5 4 3 2 1 WKT

I Am Cat!

Peter Bently

Chris Chatterton

Penguin Workshop

I am Cat.
Cat is me.

A most superior thing to be.

I like stretchy-stretchy paws.

I like scratchy-scratchy claws.

Cat is hungry.

Pad,
pad,
pad.

Human sleeping.
That's too bad.

Hello, human!
This way now.

Purr-purr. Purr-purr.
Rumbling tum.

Oops! No stumbling!
Purr. Munch. Yum.

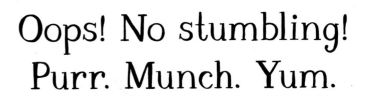

I am Cat.
I roam and prowl.
HISS! Intruder!
HISS! HISS!

YOWL!

Good.
No more intruders here.

I am Cat.
I have no fear.

Tiger, tiger stalking prey.
Hunting, hunting night and day.

Something moving. Mouse or frog?
Bird? Or toad? Or—

Next-door dog!

I am Cat. Bird I see.
Leopard, leopard up the tree.

Bird up. Cat up.
Bird up. Cat.

Bird. Cat.

I am Cat. Ignore the crowd.
Lion, lion fierce and proud.

Lick-lick.
Lick-lick.
Here.

And there.

Lick-lick.
Lick-lick.
Everywhere.

Every day is Cat fun day.
Little human wants to play.

This way. That way.
This way. That.

This way…
Gotcha!
I am Cat!

Dog bed?

Lap!

I am Cat. I love to hug.
Purr-purr.
Purr-purr.

Warm and
snug.

Little human strokes my fur.
Ears. Chin. Tummy.
Purr-purr purr.

Me time.

Stretchy-stretch on mat.
Snooze till dinnertime.

I am Cat.